D0596976

JF
EI

#3

HITTY'S TRAVELS

Voting Rights Days

ELLEN WEISS

ILLUSTRATED BY BETINA OGDEN

ALADDIN PAPERBACKS

New York   London   Toronto   Sydney   Singapore

The author wishes to acknowledge her great debt to Doris Stevens,
courageous author of *Jailed for Freedom*, which provided much
valuable background material for this book.

First Aladdin Paperbacks edition March 2002
Text copyright © 2002 by Simon & Schuster
Illustrations copyright © 2002 by Betina Ogden

Aladdin Paperbacks
An imprint of Simon & Schuster
Children's Publishing Division
1230 Avenue of the Americas
New York, NY 10020

Designed by Debra Sfetsios
The text of this book was set in Celestia Antiqua
Printed and bound in the United States of America

2 4 6 8 10 9 7 5 3 1

Library of Congress Control Number for Library Edition: 2001093282

ISBN 0-689-84912-5

CHAPTER ONE

Christmas 1916

"You can open your eyes now, Emily."

The eyes of the little girl before me had been scrunched up tight. But now she had them opened wide. They grew wider still when she saw me.

"It's a doll!" she cried. "A beautiful, beautiful doll! Just what I wanted so much for Christmas! Oh, thank you, Mama! Thank you, Papa!"

"Her name is Hitty," said Emily's mother.

"How do you know?" Emily asked.

"Take a peek at her slip. You'll see that her name is cross-stitched there in red thread."

Emily carefully lifted up the lovely new red taffeta dress I was wearing. Her mother had had the dress specially made for me at a fancy shop downtown. "There it is!" she said. "'Hitty!' I wonder who sewed it there?"

"She's quite old. I imagine we'll never know," said Emily's mother.

I knew, of course. I remembered it as if it had been yesterday. But it had been almost ninety years since Phoebe Preble had embroidered my name onto the delicate material. Ninety years since an old peddler had made me specially for Phoebe. He'd carved me out of wood from a strong mountain-ash tree. He said that mountain ash was a lucky wood. Perhaps it was, for I'd had quite a wonderful life so far. I had belonged to many girls and had been all over the world. Though I am old, my heart is still young.

But as Emily hugged me, there was something I did not yet know: In my own small way, I was about to help change history.

Emily sat me down under the enormous Christmas tree. I took the opportunity to look about me. My mountain-ash luck had really held this time. I had landed in a large, comfortable home in Washington, D.C., the nation's capital. I was to be part of the Bryan family, a loving clan with three curly-haired daughters, ages ten, nine, and six. Mr. Bryan was a lawyer, and he seemed to be a successful one. There was no want here, and no strife.

"Emily, can I play with her?" chirped the youngest sister.

"Maybe tonight, Sarah," said Emily. "I have to have her to myself for a *little* while, don't I?"

"Sarah," said Maria, "you just got a lovely new tea set. Don't you want to play with that for a while?" Maria, the eldest, seemed to be the voice of reason.

"I want to play with Hitty *and* the tea set." Sarah pouted.

"Well, maybe we could have a nice tea party later," said Emily. "I'll bring Hitty. Maria will bring her new teddy bear, and you'll serve the tea. All right, Sarah?"

"Hooray!" said Sarah, jumping up and down.

Meanwhile their mother was opening a gift wrapped in Japanese cloth.

"Your sister Ada always gives you such beautiful things," said Mr. Bryan. "Even if she is always ranting and raving about women voting, she does have good taste."

His wife shot him a look. Then she returned to her gift. "Oh, look, it's a book! The writings of Mr. Henry David Thoreau! Well, I've always wanted to curl up with this book!"

"I'll take a turn when you're finished," said her husband. He smiled. "Otherwise, I'll be jealous of you and Mr. Thoreau."

"Not much point in that, Arthur, since he's been dead for a good fifty years," laughed Mrs.

Bryan. "And now, aren't you going to open your present? The girls and I picked it out."

"Well, then it must be just awful," he said.

I was just beginning to figure out that Mr. Bryan joked all the time. It had taken me a bit of getting used to, for I had never met someone like him. But he made his family laugh every minute. They certainly understood that he meant only to amuse them.

Mr. Bryan opened the box. "Why, it's a beautiful pair of kidskin gloves!" he exclaimed.

"They're for when you're driving your motorcar!" said Sarah. "They're driving gloves!"

"They're completely wonderful," he said, pulling them on. "They fit perfectly." He seemed to be too happy even to make a joke.

"Papa, can we take a ride right now?" asked Emily.

"Well . . .," he mused. "It isn't very cold out. Molly, my dear, do you think we have time to take old Betsy out for a spin before dinner?" he asked his wife. "We could just drive down and take a look at the Potomac."

"Yes! The river!" Maria joined in. "The river on Christmas day!"

Mrs. Bryan smiled. "I suppose we could," she said. "A short one. Cook put the turkey in the oven only half an hour ago."

And so, out we went. Emily did not want to leave me behind. Maria brought her bear as well. Mrs. Bryan and the girls had all put on hats. The hats were tied on with scarves to keep the wind from blowing them away. I, myself, was worried about my lovely, big red hat. It had dozens of tiny silk roses on it. I could only hope that the dressmaker had pinned it firmly onto my hair.

Mr. Bryan's Ford was standing on the big circular driveway of the great yellow house on Newark Street. Perhaps the most amazing change I had seen in my lifetime was this business of automobiles. Just a few years before this, almost nobody had them. They were toys for a handful of very wealthy people. Now it seemed almost everyone in America had one. New roads had to be built, just for the motorcars. The Bryans' car was large and open, with room enough to seat everyone. We all climbed in, except for Mr. Bryan. He knelt down and began turning the crank to start it.

"Please be careful, darling," said Mrs. Bryan from inside the car. "You know how that crank kicks when the engine catches. I'm so afraid it's going to hit you. Mrs. Browning's husband was badly hurt last week. I don't know why you won't buy a new car. One with one of those electric starters. It's so much easier and safer."

"Yes, then Mama could drive it too!" said Maria.

"Old Betsy is a perfectly good car." Mr. Bryan grunted. "I don't see why I need to rush out and buy a new one. You just . . . need to know . . . the trick to holding the crank." Now he was sweating. "Thumb wrapped around index finger, so you can—" Suddenly the engine caught. A great puff of black smoke coughed out the back of the car. The crank lurched, and he jumped aside just in time.

"There," he said. "Nothing to it." He removed the crank and climbed in behind the wheel.

We bumped out of the cobblestone driveway and down the street. Mr. Bryan was as happy as a clam. Every time he saw a neighbor driving by, he would squeeze the bulb that honked the horn. They would honk back and wave. Past Rock Creek Park we went, all the trees bare and gray. Over the ruts and stones we rattled. At times, I was afraid my head would be shaken loose from my body! The solid rubber tires were very good, I knew, but they certainly did not cushion our ride one bit. I was glad that at least it was not nighttime. Mr. Bryan would not have to light up the smelly kerosene headlamps.

"Mama," said Maria. "I saw an advertisement in the newspaper last week for the new model cars. You should see what they are coming out with this year! They have all kinds of details for ladies. There are crystal flower vases. There are vanity cases that have smelling salts in case you faint. And there are even clocks! Wouldn't that be nice to have?"

"I don't need all those fancy things." Mrs. Bryan smiled. "I'm certainly not going to faint. But I have been thinking that I would like to be able to drive a car. It would give me much more independence. I could go where I like, when I like."

Mr. Bryan snorted. "Independence, my eye. Don't you have enough independence already? You know I love you more than life itself. Anything you want, I can buy you!"

Mrs. Bryan just sighed. She did not say anything for a long time.

The wish for independence was certainly something I could understand. I had had quite a bit of independence, for a doll. I had, after all, seen a good deal of the world. But I was always at the whim of the Fates. Like Mrs. Bryan, I sometimes wished I could go where I liked, when I liked.

At any rate, it was Christmas. And so, by the time we returned home, Mrs. Bryan's good cheer had returned. She helped Cook lay out the holiday dinner, and we had a very festive meal.

From my perch in Emily's lap, though, I could see that Emily was looking at her mother often. There was nothing, I was beginning to feel, that Emily missed. Perhaps it was because she was the middle child. Sarah was the little one. Maria was the grown-up, responsible one. And Emily? She watched.

CHAPTER TWO

Ada

No more was said about the motorcar idea. But it caused me to think quite a bit. Mrs. Bryan certainly did have everything her husband could buy her. Or, at least, everything that her husband thought she should have. Why, then, could she not have the thing she wanted most? She wanted the independence that driving a car would give her. Why was he against her having this independence?

One evening in February the doorbell rang. Mr. Bryan was not yet home from work. The rest of us were sitting in the parlor. Emily had propped me on a pillow beside her on the sofa. Her mother was helping her with her schoolwork.

Sarah ran to get the door. "It's Aunt Ada! It's Aunt Ada!" she shouted, running into the parlor. Right behind her was a tall, striking woman. She had the same flaming red hair as Emily. Mrs. Bryan, Emily, and Maria jumped up and hugged her. "Why, what a wonderful surprise!" Mrs. Bryan said. "If I knew you were coming, I'd have waited dinner—"

"No, no," said Aunt Ada. "No need at all. I was just passing by, so I thought I'd stop in. Is it all right? Are you busy?"

"Of course not," said Mrs. Bryan. "I was just helping Emily with her lessons. History."

Emily made a face. History, I already knew, was not her favorite subject. She liked art much better.

"History, eh?" said Aunt Ada. "Well, Emily, can you tell me who is going to be inaugurated as our next president soon?"

"That's easy," said Emily. "It's Woodrow Wilson. Again."

"Right you are!" said Aunt Ada. "Another four years of Woodrow Wilson. And do you know what extra-special thing will be happening in March on Inauguration Day?"

Emily furrowed her brows. "I don't think we learned that, Aunt Ada," she said. "What is it?"

"Your Aunt Ada is going to be marching with lots of other women to the White House."

"I know!" Sarah broke in. "You're marching for suffering, right?"

Aunt Ada laughed. "Not exactly," she said. "Really, we're marching to *end* our suffering. We're trying to win the right to vote. It's called 'suffrage.' Women's suffrage."

"So," said Mrs. Bryan, "you're planning another march? Will it be like the one we had on President Wilson's first inauguration?"

"Do you remember how grand that was, Molly?" said Aunt Ada. "There were eight thousand of us!"

"I do, indeed, remember," said Mrs. Bryan. "I marched with a banner that said, VOTES FOR WOMEN! And right up at the front, with the organizers, was my little sister. I'm so proud of you. You've been working so hard for the rest of us."

Just the night before, Emily and her mother had been speaking about Aunt Ada. I had listened with great interest and learned a great deal. Ada had devoted her life to winning the vote for women. She traveled constantly, giving speeches, marching, and writing articles. She had even met the president. Living on very little money, Ada often slept in the homes of supporters and ate when she had time.

"How did she get to be the way she is?" Emily had asked her mother.

Mrs. Bryan thought about it. "You know, I think she was just born that way. She always cared so much about justice and fairness. Even when she was a little girl, younger than you.

And she always thought girls were just as smart as boys."

"Well, they are," said Emily.

I had certainly found that to be true myself. Most of the girls who had owned me had had very quick minds. And, if I do say so myself, I felt that I was quite a bit brighter than the toy soldiers I had met.

"And that's why Aunt Ada spends her time working for suffrage now," Emily's mother had said. "Because women are smart enough to vote."

The suffragettes had started their own political party, Mrs. Bryan had explained. Now there were the Republicans, the Democrats, and the National Woman's Party. The National Woman's Party existed for only one cause: to win the right for women to vote. Alice Paul was elected to head the party. She was a small, dark, intense, and pretty woman. Everyone called her Miss Paul. And Aunt Ada was one of her close advisers.

Recently, these suffragettes had begun picketing the White House. They stood in front of the gates, silently holding signs. MR. PRESIDENT, said some of them, HOW LONG MUST WOMEN WAIT FOR LIBERTY?

Mr. Bryan liked to tease his sister-in-law about getting married and settling down. "There's a new fellow in my office," he would say. "*Very* nice-looking." But Ada always laughed. She would think about getting married when her work was done, she said.

"The march this year will be different," Ada now explained to her sister. "We will have a thousand women holding banners. They are all members of our new party. We will bring a list of our ideas to President Wilson. We absolutely must get him to listen to us. It's so urgent now."

"Why now?" Maria asked.

"We are about to enter the Great War at any moment," Ada explained. "But half of the country—the women—have had no say in it. Mothers will have to send their sons off to a war they never voted for."

I had heard about this war. Wherever Emily took me—at school, at home, in shops—people were talking about it. It had already been raging in Europe for over two years. It was a terrible war. Half the world seemed to be fighting in it. It was very hard to understand what they were fighting this war over. Perhaps they did not really know, either.

"Molly," Aunt Ada urged her sister, "come and watch us march! We need your support. Maybe you can even bring the girls."

Mrs. Bryan bit her lip. "You know Arthur almost had a fit the last time I marched," she said. "It's not that he doesn't think women should vote. He just thinks it's not ladylike for women to be out in the streets with banners. He thinks we should wait until Mr. Wilson decides to do what is right."

"Hah!" said Aunt Ada. "Not in *this* lifetime! We have been pleading with him for four years. All he ever says is, 'I'll think about it.' We're tired of asking politely. We're tired of begging for our rights."

"We'd like to cheer you on," said Mrs. Bryan. "I'll try to come."

"Well, you'd certainly be a welcome sight," said Aunt Ada. "I hope you can come."

March 4, Inauguration Day, dawned gray and raw. Mrs. Bryan had decided to go to the march. She would take her two older girls to lend the marchers support. They would carry jugs of hot soup and tea for those who were hungry and cold.

"It's a bad day for a march," said Mr. Bryan, looking out the window. "I think you're as crazy as they are. It looks like it will rain. You'll catch cold."

"It's important," his wife replied. "We'll take our umbrellas."

Emily and Maria were bundled up warmly. Emily bundled me up as well. She dressed me in a brown woolen coat that she had taken off one of her old dolls. It did not fit well, but I was rather glad to have it. My joints tended to swell when I got soaked.

"Off to save the universe?" Mr. Bryan asked Emily as we were packing up.

"Yes, Papa," she giggled. "When we get home, the universe will be saved."

"Well, thank goodness," he replied. He ruffled her hair. "Try not to get too wet."

When we got out the door, a bitter wind hit us squarely in our faces. We leaned into it as we walked to the streetcar stop on Connecticut Avenue.

By the time we got off the streetcar, a stinging rain had begun to fall. There was already a huge crowd lined up to watch the march. Most of the spectators stood under large umbrellas. Many of them were women, but a few were men. We took our place not far from the White House gates.

The marchers did not carry umbrellas, because each of them carried a heavy banner. The banners were purple, gold, and white, the suffragettes' colors. I watched as they fought their way into the gale. Icy water ran down the poles, soaking the sleeves of their dresses up to the elbows. Their shoes made squishing sounds as they walked. But they kept marching, heads held high. Some of the women were young, some were old, others were strong, and still others were weak. Their banners showed that they came from all over the country.

"You keep up the fight!" called out one woman. "We need the vote!"

"The men don't keep us from going to war!" shouted another one. "It's our turn to try now!"

One man in a straw hat stepped out of the crowd. "Go home!" he shouted. "Take care of your children!" Then he threw something, hard. It landed with a *splat* on a woman's shoulder. It was a rotten tomato.

The woman, who looked like a grandmother, simply wiped off the tomato and kept on marching. She lost not a speck of dignity. Emily and Maria crowded a bit closer to their mother.

"Shame on you!" the women in the crowd shouted at the tomato-throwing man.

"He's right!" yelled a woman. "This is a time for everyone to rally around President Wilson. You shouldn't be causing trouble now. A war is coming!"

"It's not our war!" one woman shouted back. "We didn't vote for it! We just have to lose our husbands to it!"

Of course, it wasn't my war, either. I was only a doll, and I could never vote in any case. But it seemed to me that women should be able to vote. After all, the laws made by those men in Washington, D.C., touched women's lives in a thousand ways.

As the argument raged on in the crowd, I noticed that the marchers had slowed down. I could see Ada's flaming hair at the head of the line.

"Hold up!" someone near Ada yelled. "Time to stop! Miss Paul is going in to give the president our list of demands!"

The line of marchers slowly halted. The rain had turned to sleet.

At the front of the line, I began to hear a great hubbub. Emily stood on tiptoe to see, but the crowd was very thick.

"You can't go in there," said a man's voice. "The gates are locked."

"But we informed the president that we were coming." That was Ada's voice.

"Sorry. You can't go in."

"Then we'll try the next gate."

The group began to move again, toward the second gate. "Mama, can we go too? I want to see what happens!" begged Emily.

"All right," said Mrs. Bryan. "Just make sure you're hanging on to me. I don't want to lose you in this crowd."

We made our way through the crowd. Emily and Maria kept jumping up to see.

It was not difficult, however, to figure out what was happening at the next gate. I could only see the back of the man in front of me. But I could hear, clear as a bell.

"You can't come in here, Miss," said the guard. "Gate's locked."

"Well, then, we'll go to the third gate."

On they pushed, with Mrs. Bryan and her daughters threading through the crowd to follow. But it was the same story again. "This gate's locked, Miss."

The National Woman's Party was not giving up so easily. "We'll wait here until the president agrees to see us," said Ada. "The rest of the group will keep on moving around the White House."

So the endless column of women began slowly circling the White House again. We stayed near Miss Paul's group to see what would happen. Pulling on her mother's skirt, Emily worked her way to the front. Now I could see well.

"Sir," said Alice Paul to the guard, "please go inside and let the president's secretary know that we are here. Tell him we request to see the president. If you would be so kind."

"All right, Miss. I'll see what I can do," said

the guard. Then he bent down closer to her. "You know, a lot of us support your cause," he said quietly. "You should be able to vote."

"Thank you," she said.

In five minutes he was back.

"What happened?" Miss Paul asked.

"I got into trouble for leaving my post," he said. He did not look happy.

"Look!" cried Maria. She was pointing up, toward the windows of the White House offices.

We all looked up, following her finger. There in the windows were some pasty faces. They belonged to clerks who worked in the White House. They were looking down at the marchers. Many of them were smirking.

Four times, the line of women circled the White House. Four times in the freezing rain. And still there was no word from inside. The rain beat down on our umbrellas.

At last, late in the afternoon, the front gates

opened. Out glided a long limousine. With some effort I caught a glimpse inside. There on the back seat was President Wilson. He looked neither left nor right, but straight ahead. He would not meet the eyes of the marchers, nor anyone in the crowd. He could have received Miss Paul and Ada and the others for a few moments. But he had chosen not to. The crowd parted, and he was gone.

There were many people that day who got a look into that car. I saw their faces harden into bitterness. I could almost feel their hearts harden as well.

CHAPTER THREE

For Shame!

On April 7 the United States officially entered the Great War. President Wilson had tried to keep the country out of it. But in the end, he could not.

Aunt Ada had been picketing at the gates of the White House every day for weeks. Mrs. Bryan and the girls often carried food there for Ada and the other women. Emily always took me along. She was becoming more and more excited about Ada's cause.

One day Ada told us that two of her friends had been arrested the day before.

"Oh, my goodness!" cried Mrs. Bryan. "What happened to them?"

"Well," said Ada, "the police had a hard time thinking what to accuse them of. Picketing is perfectly legal. The best they could come up with was blocking traffic." She took a sip of Mrs. Bryan's piping hot bean soup.

"That's ridiculous!" said Emily. "You aren't even blocking traffic!"

"Quite right," laughed Ada. "They had to let them go the same day."

"But Ada," said her sister. "What will you do if they arrest *you*?"

"We'll just have to take that as it comes," said Ada. "But I'm certainly not breaking any laws."

"You are making quite a few people angry, though," said Mrs. Bryan. "I've read that some suffragettes have decided to stop their fight while the war is on. They're helping the soldiers, instead."

"They are doing good work, too," said Ada. "our group has split from theirs. We believe even more strongly that we must have the vote now. After all, England and Russia are giving their women the right to vote. It's wartime for them, too. And they are fighting on our side. Some of our group agree with the president about this war, and some don't. But that's not the point. The point is that we must have some say in it."

"I just hope you don't get arrested." Maria fretted. "I don't want you to go to jail!"

"Don't you worry," said Aunt Ada.

Just then a huge, red-faced man came rushing up to Ada. "You!" he yelled. "What kind of women are you? Troublemakers! Well, I'll give you some trouble!"

To our great alarm he lunged at Aunt Ada. He was trying to snatch off the sash she was wearing across her chest. In a flash Emily stepped in front of her aunt. "Don't you touch her!" she cried.

"Emily!" shrieked her mother.

The man was too enraged to think clearly. "Get out of my way!" he yelled.

"No!" said Emily. She thrust me out in front of her for protection.

The man grabbed at me. Emily held on. My arms and legs were being pulled in two directions. "Oh, please, let my life not end here!" I prayed.

We had scarcely noticed it, but across the street, a photographer had been setting up his camera. He had probably been planning to take a simple photo of the picket line. But he seemed to have finished setting up at just the right moment. A sudden flash blinded us all for a second. Startled, the man let go of me.

"Got it!" the photographer shouted.

The next morning there was a large headline on the front page of the morning newspaper. FOR SHAME! it shouted. Below the headline was a photograph. There was Emily, standing bravely between her aunt and the attacking man. There were Aunt Ada and Mrs. Bryan and Maria, trying to stop him. And there was poor little me in the middle, being almost torn in half.

"There is no excuse for this brutal attack," said the newspaper. "No matter how we feel about the matter of women voting, we cannot become animals. Are we now attacking little girls and dolls?"

Mr. Bryan read the article aloud over breakfast. "Well, Hitty," he said to me, "I guess you're the heroine of the day. Why didn't you tell us you were such a firebrand?"

Emily laughed at what her father had said. "Hitty protected me and Aunt Ada," she said. "My brave little doll!"

"You were very brave yourself," said Mrs. Bryan. "Though I don't ever want you to do that again. You could have been hit by that man!"

I, too, was amazed at Emily's bravery. It was a

part of her that I had not seen before. When she needed to, she could be as tough as her Aunt Ada.

"I would have hit him right back," said Emily. "Or maybe bitten him on the arm."

"My goodness!" said Mr. Bryan. "Well, I must say, I am beginning to change my mind about the picketing. If men like that one are against it, then I think I must be for it."

"Well said, my dear!" said Mrs. Bryan.

"Though I'm still not very crazy about these women marching around like mechanical soldiers," he added.

"A true lady, in my opinion, is not just some fragile little flower," said Mrs. Bryan. "A true lady fights for justice."

"I would like to propose a toast," said Maria. She held up her glass of orange juice. "To Hitty. She is our own little fighter for justice. *And* she is a true lady."

"Hear, hear!" said Mr. Bryan. Emily lifted me

high above the table, and they all clinked glasses below me. I felt very honored. I realized at that moment that the cause of women's suffrage had become my cause.

The attacks on the picketers did not end. They just grew worse. It was amazing to me that the simple wish to cast a vote could cause such rage. But rage was what the picketers had to withstand. The police began arresting women again. The charge was still blocking traffic. But now the sentences were severe. In July, sixteen women, including some grandmothers, were sentenced to sixty days in the workhouse.

Luckily, the newspapers made a fuss about it. On the third day the women were pardoned by the president and sent home. "We do not need a pardon," the women told the newspapers. "We did nothing wrong."

By August millions of men had been sent off

to the war. We were grateful that Mr. Bryan did not have to report to the army. Younger men without children were the first to go.

The suffragettes did not stop picketing. That made some people even angrier. Now there were riots against the women. The police were supposed to be keeping the peace, but they attacked the picketers. Alice Paul was knocked down three times. More women were arrested.

I did not see Aunt Ada for quite awhile. She was much too busy to visit her sister's house. Mrs. Bryan often went down to the White House to bring the picketers food and drink. But she did not take the girls anymore. It was just too dangerous.

She would come home with interesting reports, however. The girls listened hungrily to every detail. And so did I. "Today was 'College Day' on the picket line," Mrs. Bryan said one day. "There were dozens of college women lined up.

Each one wore a banner with the name of her college on it—Vassar, Swarthmore, the University of Missouri—oh, it went on and on!"

"I'm going to college when I grow up!" said Sarah. "Then I can be a picketer too."

"I hope that women won't still be picketing the White House by that time!" exclaimed her mother. "Perhaps when you finish college, you can be president, instead."

"All right," said Sarah. "I'll be president."

On other days Mrs. Bryan reported that the picket line had featured different professions. There were teachers and nurses, factory workers and lawyers.

"Well, did you and Ada save the universe today?" Mr. Bryan would often ask at dinner.

"Perhaps just one corner of it," his wife would reply with a tired smile.

"Mama, are you going to join the picketers?" Emily asked one day.

A cloud passed over her mother's face. "I would dearly love to," she said. "But what if I got arrested? What if I were taken to jail? Who would take care of you girls?"

"Besides," said Mr. Bryan, "where would the picketers get their bean soup?"

Just before dessert the doorbell rang. "I bet it's Aunt Ada!" cried Sarah. "I'll go get it!"

But when she returned, she was leading a young woman whom the Bryan family did not know. A look of fear immediately passed over Mrs. Bryan's face. "It's Ada, isn't it?" she said, without even waiting for introductions.

"I'm afraid it is," said the young woman. "My name is Jane. I have been picketing with Ada."

"I thought I recognized you," said Mrs. Bryan. "What's happened?"

"Ada asked me to come and tell you that she has been arrested," said Jane.

Mrs. Bryan got very pale and looked as if she

were about to faint. Then she recovered. "Please, sit down," she said. "Take some tea with us. Tell us what happened."

Jane sat down. "Thank you," she said. "I am rather tired, I must admit."

"Have you eaten dinner?" asked Mr. Bryan.

"Oh, goodness, I forgot to eat," she said. "There was just too much excitement."

Jane was promptly given some dinner. As she gratefully ate it she told the family what had happened. "About eleven of us were arrested late this afternoon," she said. "Everyone was taken to the station house. For some reason, they let me go. Maybe I looked too young. But Ada and the others have been held. They will be tried very quickly, probably tomorrow. If you want to see the trial, you probably can. But there won't be anything you can do. The judge will give them thirty or sixty days in jail, unless they pay a fine. But they won't agree to pay the fine, of course. We haven't done anything wrong."

"Do they have a lawyer?" asked Mr. Bryan worriedly.

"Yes, the Party has a lawyer," Jane explained. "He's quite busy these days. So many women are being arrested. But he won't be able to do much. If you want to say good-bye to Ada, you'd better go to court tomorrow."

Mrs. Bryan looked as if someone had hit her across the face. The girls' eyes were brimming with tears.

"Maybe there's something I can do," said Mr. Bryan.

"Yes, please try, Papa!" said Emily. "Please! Maybe someone at your law office knows the judge or something!"

"I'll try," he said.

CHAPTER FOUR

Occoquan

Mr. Bryan called all the important people he knew. But there was nothing he could do. There was nothing anyone could do.

The courtroom was packed with worried families and friends. There were also several reporters there. The girls had begged to go, so they could see their aunt before she was sent away. Once again, Sarah was left at home. Her mother felt it would be too upsetting for one so young. Mr. Bryan was there. He had left his office to attend the court session.

Emily brought me along, and I was glad. I wanted to see for myself what would happen. I could not bear to think of beautiful, spirited Ada being locked up in jail. There she was, standing tall in the prisoners' dock, along with her friends. She looked tired and hungry. There were dark circles under her eyes. But she looked the judge straight in the eye and did not look away.

It was over very quickly. First there was some legal mumbo jumbo, which I did not understand. Then the judge spoke to the women. "Do you have anything to say in your own defense?" he asked each woman. He was bald and wrinkled, with icy blue eyes.

"Men made the laws that put me here today," said the first woman. "I was not allowed to vote for these men. Why, then, should I respect this court?" Her voice was strong.

"We have broken no law," said Ada. "We have harmed no one. The charge is ridiculous, and I think you know it yourself, Your Honor. Sending women to prison for blocking traffic! I just hope you can sleep well tonight."

"Will you pay the fine instead of being sent to jail?" he asked her.

"Of course not," she replied.

He banged his heavy wooden gavel down onto his bench. "Sixty days in the workhouse at Occoquan," he said.

Mrs. Bryan gasped. But Ada was silent. She just set her jaw a bit harder. As she was led out of the courtroom she smiled at her sister and nieces. "I'll be out before you know it," she whispered.

The workhouse! I was still reeling from the word. It sounded like the worst place on earth. At least, I hoped, we would be able to visit Ada a lot.

As soon as we got home Mrs. Bryan set about trying to find out how we could see Ada. She stood before the oak telephone that hung on the wall in the parlor. The earpiece was held up to her ear. "Hello!" she shouted into the black mouthpiece on the phone box. "Get me the Occoquan Workhouse, please! Yes, the Occoquan Workhouse!"

As the hours wore on she became more and more frustrated. She was hoarse from shouting.

Finally, at about eight o'clock, Cook put some dinner on the table. Exhausted, Mrs. Bryan sat down with the rest of us at the table. She picked at her food.

"No luck in getting through?" said Mr. Bryan.

"None at all," she replied. "I'm not sure if they even have a phone there."

"If you write a letter," he suggested, "I'll mail it special delivery from the office. I'll see to it that it gets there in a day or two."

She sighed. "All right," she said. "Thank you. I guess a letter may be the best we can do."

She sat up late into the evening writing the letter. After the girls were put to bed, I could see the light from the downstairs parlor. The house was quiet.

Each of the three girls had a bedroom to herself. Usually, though, they all slept in the same room. They got lonely in their separate rooms.

Emily's bed was in the corner, under the big bay window. She waited until Maria and Sarah were sleeping. Then she sat up. She held me in her lap.

"Oh, Hitty," she whispered to me, "I'm so worried. Why can't Mama speak to Aunt Ada on the phone?"

I did not feel any less worried than she did. What was the workhouse like? What kind of work would Ada have to do? I knew she was strong. But was she strong enough for this?

And when would we be able to get news of her?

Day after day went by. Mrs. Bryan sent her sister a letter each and every morning. Most days the letters had drawings or notes from the girls tucked in. They all went out special delivery, from Mr. Bryan's office. But there was never a reply.

Finally, after almost two weeks, Mrs. Bryan was able to place a phone call to the workhouse. She had learned where it was located. It was in Virginia, some twenty miles to the southwest. She had a short conversation with someone there. We, of course, could only hear her end of the conversation. Mostly she said, "Pardon me?" and, "What? I couldn't hear you!" But toward the end she said, "Oh, then we'll be allowed to visit on Thursday? Very good. Thank you."

She hung up the phone. The three girls were already jumping up and down. Emily, who was holding me, was jumping so hard, I was getting dizzy. "We can visit! We can visit!" they were all shouting.

"Now, girls, I don't know if it's a good place

for children to go," said Mrs. Bryan. "I don't even know if you're allowed. Maybe your father and I should go alone."

"Pleeeeease?" they all began to beg at once. "Please, Mama! We need to see her!"

"Well," said Mr. Bryan, "I suppose we could take the girls. If they can't visit, they can wait in the car until we come out."

His wife looked a little unsure. "I suppose we could try it," she said. "If they can come in, it will make Ada very happy to see them."

On Thursday the whole family awoke very early. Before she did anything else, Emily got me ready. "You have to look extra nice for Aunt Ada," she said as she dabbed my face with a washcloth. "Let's pin your hat on better."

Emily's father went outside first, to get the car started. I could hear him cranking it in the driveway. The engine turned over in record time. It seemed to know this was no day to be difficult. Finally, at about nine o'clock, everyone was in the car. We were off.

It was a hot, muggy day. Mr. Bryan figured that the twenty-mile journey would take about an hour and a half. We bumped along, saying little. Each of us, I think, was in a private world of thought. But we were all thinking the same things. What would we find at the Occoquan Workhouse? How would Ada look? What kind of justice was there in a world where people went to jail for wanting to vote?

Mrs. Bryan had packed up a large picnic basket. It was filled with good things for Ada and her friends. There were mince pies, sardines in tins, and fresh fruit. And there was cold chicken, too. "At least she'll get one good meal while she's there," she said.

As we approached the workhouse we drove down a long avenue. The road was rocky and rough. Dark poplar trees loomed along the sides of the road. They made me feel as if we were in a tunnel.

And at last we were there. It was a collection of squat, ugly brick buildings. The main building looked a bit like a fortress. I felt Emily shudder a bit as we pulled up in front of it.

"You girls stay here," said Mr. Bryan. "We'll come out and get you if you're allowed in."

We sat in the car for what seemed an eternity. Emily absently plucked at my dress. At last her parents came out. They looked pale and shaken.

"They'll allow you to come in," said Mrs. Bryan. "But I'm not sure you ought to. It's an awful place in there. It may give you nightmares tonight."

"Oh, please let us go in!" cried Emily. "We've come so far, and we want to see her so much!"

"Besides," said Maria, "it cannot possibly be as bad as our imaginations will make it."

"All right, if you think you can handle it," said their mother. "But be ready. It's terrible inside."

And so, we went in.

I have never been in a place like that, and I hope never to be again. It was dark and murky inside. It smelled like some terrible combination of unwashed bodies and spoiled cabbage. The girls stayed very close to their parents. Sarah, especially, clung to her mother's skirt. We followed the prison matron down the hall to the visiting room.

As we moved along the dark hallways we began to hear, of all things, singing. It was faint, but it could not be mistaken. We strained our ears to hear. The tune was familiar. It was a song we all knew, called "Charlie, he's my Darling." But the words were different. They had been changed.

Shout the revolution
Of women, of women.

51

Shout the revolution for liberty.
Rise, glorious women of the earth,
The voiceless and the free;
United strength assures the birth
Of true democracy.

Where was this singing coming from? We could not see the singers. But they were somewhere, locked away behind these dark walls. And their voices, though faint, were full of spirit.

At last we reached the visiting room. No attempt had been made to make the visitors feel comfortable. It was a dark room, with one tiny window high up near the ceiling. There were a few scratched-up tables in the room. Each table had four or five rickety chairs around it.

The large female guard, who was called a matron, stopped us. "I'll have to search you," she said.

"Search us?" said Mrs. Bryan. "Whatever for?"

"Knives. Firearms. Forbidden reading material."

"Good lord!" said Mr. Bryan.

The woman did not reply. She simply patted all the Bryans up and down—even Sarah. It was absolutely shocking. Emily held tightly onto me. Luckily, the woman did not search me. I think it would have been more than I could bear!

Then the matron looked inside the picnic basket.

"There are no firearms in it," said Mrs. Bryan in a chilly tone.

"I'll still have to take it away," said the guard. "No food is to be brought in."

"Why in heaven's name not?" asked Mrs. Bryan. "I'm sure they could use some healthy food."

"This ain't a country club." With that, the guard snapped the lid closed.

We took our seats and waited for Ada to be brought out. No one else in the workhouse seemed to have visitors on that particular Thursday. We were alone in the waiting room, except for the guard. She watched us with narrowed eyes.

"Maybe she thinks we're going to steal the chairs," whispered Mr. Bryan. Even here, he tried to find something to joke about.

After about twenty minutes Ada was brought in. If we had not expected her, we might not have recognized her.

She wore a scratchy, ill-fitting sort of thing. I could not even call it a dress. It looked pretty much like a potato sack. She limped badly. Her cheeks were hollow. Her hair, so lovely just two weeks ago, was knotted and uncombed. But when she saw us, she broke into a beautiful smile.

"They told me just an hour ago that you were

coming!" she said. "I can't believe you're really here!"

"They didn't make it easy for us," said her sister.

"Of course not," Ada replied. "They don't want people coming. Nobody is allowed any visitors for two weeks. If they're lucky."

"At least you had our letters," Mrs. Bryan said.

Ada's face fell. "So you *have* written me letters," she said.

"Every day."

"I have not gotten one of them," said Ada. Her eyes flashed in anger. "I had a feeling you must have written."

"We've been so desperate to hear news of you," said Mrs. Bryan. "How do they treat you? Are you all right?"

"We take care of each other," said Ada. "That keeps us going."

"Do you have to work, Aunt Ada?" asked Maria.

"We are supposed to be working at sewing machines," Ada replied. "But the suffragettes are refusing. We broke no law, so we won't work."

"I heard you singing," said Sarah. "Was that you?"

"Yes, my darling. It was me and the others. We sing to give each other strength. They don't let us talk to each other. But they can't stop us from singing."

"What are these clothes they have you in?" asked Mrs. Bryan.

"They took them off other prisoners and gave them to us," Ada replied. "They're not so bad. It's the shoes that are bad. They give you two shoes that are the same, made to go on either foot. They're all the same size. We all have great blisters on our feet."

"Have you been able to take a bath?"

"Only once so far. Everything smells so awful. The blankets are only washed once a year.

And all the food is full of worms. They float on the top of the soup. If soup is what it is."

The whole Bryan family gasped at once. Sarah began to cry.

"It's so horrible, Aunt Ada!" cried Emily.

"It's only for a while," said her aunt. "It will end soon. It only serves to strengthen our will. We must be able to vote for people who won't make these terrible laws."

A second guard popped her head into the doorway of our room. "Margaret," she said to our matron, "you're needed on Block A."

Margaret cast a suspicious eye at us. "I'll be back in no time at all," she said warningly.

The moment she was gone, Aunt Ada leaned over to her sister. "I wrote something for you to take out," she whispered. "I did it fast, just before you came. It's the truth about how we are being treated. Take it to the *Washington Post*. We can only write one letter a month.

And even then, I've heard they cross out almost everything. People have to know!"

"But they searched us!" whispered Mrs. Bryan. "They might search us on the way out, too."

"They didn't search Hitty!" said Emily.

Suddenly six pairs of eyes turned to me. "Hitty!" whispered Ada. "Maybe we can hide the letter somewhere on her."

"How big is it?" asked Mrs. Bryan.

"It's written on tissue paper," said Ada. "I found a scrap on the floor. I used tiny writing to fit in as much as I could. It's folded up small."

"Under her hat!" whispered Sarah. "Put it under her hat! It's pinned on!"

Quickly my hat was removed by Emily's nervous fingers. She had to finish before the matron returned! The letter was pushed down onto my head, and the hat pinned firmly back on top of it.

Emily held me up close. "I can't see it," she

reported. "It's not sticking out at all."

"Hitty gives new meaning to the saying, 'Keep it under your hat,'" said Mr. Bryan.

At that instant the heavy door swung open. In walked Margaret. She looked at us even more suspiciously than before.

"Visiting time's over," she said.

"Just a little longer!" Sarah begged.

"Time's up!" Margaret repeated.

The whole family hugged Ada tearfully. Even Mr. Bryan's eyes were damp. Ada was taken away by Margaret. But before she disappeared through the barred door, she looked back. And she looked right at me.

"Godspeed," she said.

CHAPTER FIVE

Shout the Revolution

The family was indeed searched on the way out.
But once again, nobody thought to inspect me.
As soon as we got out, we drove straight to the
offices of the *Washington Post*. We did not even
stop off at home first.

"We'd like to see the editor," said Mrs. Bryan.

"We have lots of editors," said the woman at
the front desk. "Which editor do you want?"

"Any editor!" cried Mr. Bryan. "We have
important information."

"Wait here," she said. In a few moments she
was back with a tall, thin man in shirtsleeves.
"This is Mr. Jones," she said. "He's editor of the
Metropolitan page."

"What's this all about?" he asked. He seemed annoyed to be interrupted.

"It's about *this*," said Emily. Carefully she unpinned my hat. She removed the letter and handed it to him.

"What on earth is this?" he said crankily. "It's on some sort of tissue paper. And the writing—I can barely make it out!"

"Just start reading it," said Mr. Bryan.

"Who's it from, anyway?" the editor asked.

"It was written by my sister," said Mrs. Bryan. "She is a member of the National Woman's Party. She is at this moment in the women's workhouse at Occoquan."

That got him interested. He stood there reading it, right in front of us. "One letter out a month," he said to himself. "All mail read. Blankets washed once a year. Oh, my. Worms in the soup! Oh!"

He removed his reading glasses. "This is quite a story," he said.

"It certainly is," said Mr. Bryan. "I am a lawyer. But I have never seen such injustice in my life."

"Can I hold on to this?" asked Mr. Jones.

"Will you give it back after you use it?" asked Mrs. Bryan. "I'd like to keep it."

"We'll try our best," he replied. "Right now I must give it to one of my reporters. He'll have to work fast if we're going to get it into tomorrow's edition. Wait here. He'll want to interview you about what you saw."

And so, once again, my life was mixed up with the newspapers. This time I felt that I had really been of service. When the paper came out the next day, the effect was enormous. The article quoted Ada's whole letter. And the reporter had uncovered a big surprise. It seemed the government was already investigating the Occoquan Workhouse for treating prisoners badly. The warden was a brutal man named Whittaker. Inside the workhouse, Whittaker said, the law did not matter. He was the only law.

"Everyone at the office is talking about the suffragettes," reported Mr. Bryan the next evening.

"And what are they saying?" asked Emily.

"Some people are for their cause. Some are against it. But everyone is horrified by their treatment."

"Good," Emily replied. "Now maybe they'll let them out."

Emily was wrong, sad to say. The women served their entire terms in prison. Many more women were arrested too. Aunt Ada was not released until October. The Bryans had not been able to visit her again. They had gotten only one letter from her. The only words not crossed out were "How are you?" and "I miss you very much."

On the day of her release, Mr. and Mrs. Bryan went alone to pick her up in the car. They did not know how she would look, and they did not want the girls to be upset.

The girls flocked around their parents as soon as they walked in the door. "How did she look? How is she?" they wanted to know.

"She'll be all right, with some rest and some good food," said Mrs. Bryan. "She's awfully thin. But her spirits are still strong."

"I knew it!" cried Emily.

"The women knew nothing of the article in the newspaper," said her mother. "Ada was so happy when she found out that our trick with Hitty's hat had worked!"

"And Whittaker never found out who smuggled out that letter!" said Mr. Bryan. "It wasn't for lack of trying, either."

"Good old Hitty," said Emily.

"I think the mood of the whole country is

beginning to change," said Mr. Bryan. "You mark my words. Women's right to vote will come soon."

If the mood of the country was changing, the mood of the president was not. Just days after Aunt Ada was let out, Alice Paul and a few other leaders were arrested. This time they were sentenced to seven months in a Washington, D.C., jail.

As soon as she got her strength back, Aunt Ada went right back onto the picket line. More and more women joined her. More and more were arrested. Mrs. Bryan came home with the latest news every day.

The word began to get around that Alice Paul was on a hunger strike. She and the others in the jail had decided to stop eating. They hoped this would force the government to give in and let them go. Besides, the food was so awful, it was no great loss. The jailers tried to force them to eat, but they resisted.

Many, many other women were taken to Occoquan. They all received sentences of six or seven months. They were treated even worse than Ada was. And they all decided to go on a hunger strike as well.

When their lawyer tried to visit them in the workhouse, he was turned away. In frustration, he went to a judge. Since the women were arrested in Washington, D.C., he said, the government had no right to put them in jail in Virginia.

When it came time to go to court, the women were brought in to appear before the judge. Many of them could not walk. They looked terrible. They were refusing to eat, and they were being treated very badly.

But this time, it was impossible to keep the public from finding out how bad it was.

Newspaper reporters went back to their papers and wrote about what they had seen. And now things began to move quickly. There was a great public outcry. Within a very short time, all the women, including Miss Paul, were let out of jail.

And soon after that, President Wilson finally changed his mind. He decided to support the women's quest for the vote. That was all the movement needed. On June 4, 1919, the United States Congress proposed a bill for women's right to vote to the state's legislature—the Nineteenth Amendment. It was two years to the day from the time the picketers had first stood before the White House gates.

Aunt Ada was looking better and better. As the cry for suffrage got stronger throughout the country, she grew stronger too.

One day in early spring she came over to the house for lunch. She was still very busy. The vote in January had just been the beginning. There were many more obstacles to overcome before suffrage became the law. The Senate would have to vote on it, and then two-thirds of the States would have to pass the amendment as well. There was much to do.

"I have a surprise for you," Mrs. Bryan said to her sister. "It's just a little thing."

"Why, whatever is it?" asked Aunt Ada. "My birthday's not until September."

"It's just a little memento," said Mrs. Bryan. She handed Ada a pretty white box.

"Open it! Open it, Aunt Ada!" cried the girls.

Ada opened the box. There, lying on a bed of tissue paper, was my red hat.

"We were not able to retrieve your letter from the newspaper," said Mrs. Bryan, "so Emily thought you should have Hitty's hat to remember everything you've done."

"If you're ever feeling like giving up," said

Emily, "it will remind you how hard you fought back."

Aunt Ada quickly brushed a tear off her cheek. "I will treasure it," she said. "But—what will Hitty wear? She'll be hatless."

Emily ran and got me from the sofa. "Don't worry," she said. "Hitty has a new hat."

And so I did. Mrs. Bryan had ordered a very nice new red-and-white hat for me from the same dress shop. It had a tiny white feather on the side. I thought I looked quite smart.

We were interrupted by the sound of a horn being squeezed outside. "Whoever can that be?" said Maria.

"I don't know," said her mother. "Your Papa went out hours ago. I don't think he's expecting any visitors."

In a moment, the mystery was solved. The front door opened, and in walked Mr. Bryan. He looked quite cheerful. "Hello, everyone," he said. "Come outside. I have something for you, Molly."

Emily snatched me up, and we all went outside. And there in front of the house was a brand-new blue car.

"It's ours," said Mr. Bryan.

"It's really very nice," said his wife with a smile. "I'm sure you'll enjoy driving it."

"Look, Mama!" said Maria. "It has a special mirror so Papa can see the cars behind him when he's driving. That's the newest thing."

"Go and sit in it, my dear," he replied.

Looking at him quizzically, she went and sat down in her usual seat, beside the driver.

"No," he said. "I mean, in the driver's seat."

She was beginning to smile unbelievingly. "Now push that button," he said. "The red one, over there on your left. Do you see it?"

She pushed the button. The car immediately started up. The motor purred.

"This afternoon," he said, "I'll give you a driving lesson."

"I'd love that," said Mrs. Bryan.

The girls erupted into cheers. "We're coming too!" they shouted.

"Why don't you give her a name?" asked her husband.

Mrs. Bryan thought about that for a minute. "I think," she said at last, "I'll call *him* Barnaby." And then she honked the horn.

About the Fight for the Vote

Although Woodrow Wilson frustrated suffragettes and suffragists alike, historians remember him as one of our most important presidents. He tried hard to keep the United States out of the war. When that failed, he worked hard to find an end to the war, which we now call World War I. He dreamed of ending all war and started an organization that has become what we know today as the United Nations.

American women are so used to voting now, it is easy to take this right for granted. Many people have forgotten the brave women who fought so hard for so long to win it. The beginnings of the battle stretch all the way back to the 1840s.

There were many groups that worked for women's suffrage. Alice Paul's National Woman's Party was just one of them. The NAWSA, or

National American Woman Suffrage Association, did not want to picket the White House. But this group worked hard to win the vote in one state after another. They were an important part of the final victory.

In December of 1917 a huge meeting was held at the Belasco Theater in Washington. The theater was packed, and thousands of people waited outside, trying to get in. At this meeting a hundred women who had suffered the horrors of prison were given special pins. The pins were tiny silver cell doors. Each one had a fine silver chain and a heart-shaped lock. "In honoring these women, who were willing to go to jail for liberty," said the woman who fastened on their pins, "we are showing our love of country and devotion to democracy."

The Nineteenth Amendment to the Constitution, which guarantees women the right to vote, was finally passed on August 26, 1920.

Have you read the first two books in the HITTY'S TRAVELS series?

Hitty's Travels #1: Civil War Days

Hitty's owner Nell lives on a plantation in the South. When a house slave named Sarina comes to work for Nell's father, the girls become friends. But when Nell and Sarina break the rules of the plantation, things will never be the same again....

Hitty's Travels #2: Gold Rush Days

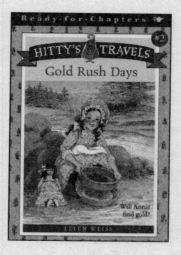

Hitty's owner Annie is excited to travel with her father to California in search of gold, but it's a tough journey out west and an even tougher life when they arrive. Annie longs to help out, but is there anything she can do?

And look for the
next book in the series!

Hitty's Travels #4: Ellis Island Days

Hitty travels to Italy in style with a spoiled little rich girl, but soon falls into the hands of Fiorella Rossi, a kind girl whose poor family longs to reach America. Will the Rossis survive the awful conditions of their long journey?